for Felix Hulbert

Distributed in the United States by Kodansha America, Inc.,
114 Fifth Avenue, New York, N.Y. 10011, and in the United
Kingdom and continental Europe by Kodansha Europe Ltd.,
Gillingham House, 38-44 Gillingham Street, London SW1V 1HU.
Published by Kodansha International Ltd., 17-14 Otowa 1-chome,
Bunkyo-ku, Tokyo 112, and Kodansha America, Inc.

93 94 95 10 9 8 7 6 5 4 3 2 1

Library of Congress Cataloging-in-Publication Data

McCarthy, Ralph F.
    Grandfather Cherry Blossom / illustrations by Eiho Hirezaki :
retold by Ralph F. McCarthy.—1st ed.
        p.   cm.—(Kodansha children's classics series : 5)
Summary: A kind old woodcutter and his greedy neighbor
are appropriately rewarded for their deeds.
    ISBN 4-7700-1759-6 :
    [1. Stories in rhyme.   2. Folklore—Japan.]   I. Hirezaki, Eiho.
1881–1968, ill.   II. Title.   III. Series.
PZ8.3.M45936Gr   1993
398.2′1′0952—dc20
[E]
                                              93-18301
                                                CIP
                                                AC

KODANSHA
CHILDREN'S CLASSICS

GRANDFATHER CHERRY-BLOSSOM

Illustrations by **Eiho Hirezaki**
Retold by **Ralph F. McCarthy**

KODANSHA INTERNATIONAL
Tokyo • New York • London

While chopping wood,
  a kind old man
Once found a dog
  who licked his hand.
He fed it something,
  named it White,
And took it home
  with him that night.

His wife said:
  "Can we keep him? Oh!
His fur's so soft,
  and white as snow!"
And so her husband,
  White and she
Became a family of three.

5

One day White howled and scratched the ground.
"What is it, White? What have you found?"
The old man said and grabbed his hoe.
"Hoe here!" White seemed to howl, and so . . .

The kind old man
    began to dig
Till he hit something
    hard and big:
It was a pot
    chock full of gold
(Which comes in handy
    when you're old).

A mean old man who lived next door
Thought *he* deserved gold even more.
He dragged White over to his field
Till White lay down and howled and squealed.

The mean man tied White to a tree
And said: "Is this the spot? Whoopee!"
He dug away the dirt and stones,
But all he found was trash and bones.

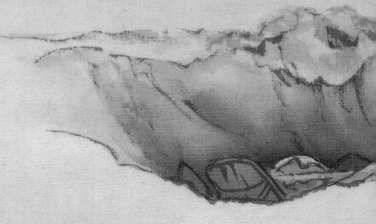

The mean old man
  was furious;
    He raised his hoe
      (that dirty cuss)
And gave poor White an awful whack
That knocked him down and broke his back.

The kind old man came on the run.
"What's this?" he cried."What have you done?"
"He bit me," lied the mean old man,
"And so I hit him. Understand?"

14

The kind old gentle man and wife
Tried hard to save the poor dog's life,
But, sad to say, their lovely White
Died in their arms that very night.

18

With heavy hearts, the kind old pair
Laid White to rest and said a prayer
And took a small pine tree they'd found
And planted it beside his mound.

The pine tree grew so fast that soon
Its branches seemed to touch the moon.
"The strangest thing I ever saw!"
The neighbors cried, and stared in awe.

The old man said: "It seems to me
White's spirit must be in this tree."

21

His wife said: "Wouldn't it be good
To carve a mortar from the wood
(Before it grows too tall and breaks),
And pound some rice to make some cakes?"

"Good thinking, dear," the man replied.
"White loved rice cakes before he died!"

And when the mortar was complete
They filled it up with rice to beat
And pound and knead
        and knead and pound,
And soon they heard
        a tinkling sound . . .

And something
    hit the floor
        and rolled—
The rice
    was turning
        into gold!

As they began to celebrate,
The mean old man came through the gate.
He eyed the mortar greedily
And said: "It's just the thing for me!
It's just what I've been looking for!"
He said, and rolled it out the door.

The mean man told
        his mean old wife:
"We'll soon be rich!
        We're set for life!"
He beat the rice, and in a flash
It all turned into bones and trash.

The mean man ran to get his axe
And gave the mortar fifty whacks;
And still his anger didn't cease—
Until he'd burned up every piece.

The kind man came and bowed his head.
"Please give my mortar back," he said.
"I burned that worthless piece of trash,"
The mean man said. "You want the ash?"

"Look, dear! He murders White, and now
He burns the mortar! Tell me, how
Can one man be so full of spite?
This ash is all that's left of White!"
The kind man moaned. Just then, a breeze
Blew ashes on some dried-up trees.
Imagine their surprise when—*zoom!*
The dead trees all burst into bloom!

"The ash makes
dead trees bloom again!"
The kind old man
was shouting, when
A young prince
from the castle town
Rode by and
stopped him with a frown.

"Dead trees can't bloom!" the young prince said.
"Old man, you should be home in bed."

"It's true, I swear, Your Majesty.
I'll show you if you'd like to see!"

"I would indeed," the young prince laughed.
"You're either very wise—or daft!"

The kind man climbed a cherry tree
And sprinkled ashes. Suddenly
A thousand cherry-blooms appeared.
"Hooray! Hooray!" the young prince cheered.

The prince said: "Sir, I'm in your debt.
Please take this sack of gold, and let
Grandfather Cherry-Blossom be
The title I bestow on thee."

The mean old woman overheard
And told her man what had occurred:
"A title and a sack of cash!
For sprinkling a little ash
Upon a withered cherry tree!
If *he* can do it, so can we.
Scoop up those ashes! Go, I say!
Before the prince can ride away!"

42

The mean old man climbed up a tree
And waited there till he could see
The prince approaching on his horse,
Then threw the ashes, but of course
No blooms appeared. A breeze again
Blew up and blew the ashes in
The prince's face, and on his clothes,
And in his mouth, and up his nose.

"Arrest that man!" the young prince sneezed.
They threw the mean man to his knees
And tied him up and dragged him off.
"For disrespect!" the young prince coughed.

And so the mean man went to jail,
And that's the end of White's fine tale.
(Oh, yes—the kind old man and wife?
They lived a long and happy life.)

KODANSHA CHILDREN'S CLASSICS

THE ADVENTURES OF MOMOTARO, THE PEACH BOY
Illustrations by Ioe Saito
Retold by Ralph F. McCarthy

THE MOON PRINCESS
Illustrations by Kancho Oda
Retold by Ralph F. McCarthy

URASHIMA AND THE KINGDOM BENEATH THE SEA
Illustrations by Shiro Kasamatsu
Retold by Ralph F. McCarthy

THE INCH-HIGH SAMURAI
Illustrations by Shiro Kasamatsu
Retold by Ralph F. McCarthy

GRANDFATHER CHERRY-BLOSSOM
Illustrations by Eiho Hirezaki
Retold by Ralph F. McCarthy

DATE DUE

SEP 27 1994			
MAY 05 1998			
GAYLORD			PRINTED IN U.S.A.